Oliver Moon and the Dragon Disaster

Sue Mongredien

Illustrated by
Jan McCafferty

USBORNE

For James Brothwell, with lots of love

First published in 2006 by Usborne Publishing Ltd., Usborne House,
83-85 Saffron Hill, London EC1N 8RT, England. usborne.com

A CIP catalogue record for this book is available from
the British Library.

JFMAMJJA OND/20   02822/4

ISBN 9780746073070

Printed in India

Contents

Chapter One

Oliver Moon was soaring on his
broomstick, high above Magic School.
All his friends and teachers were down
below in the playground, watching him.
"Oooh," they chorused as Oliver loop-
the-looped twice in a row.

"Wow!" they breathed as he zipped
backwards, both hands high in the air.

"Hooray!" they cheered, as he zigzagged through the tanglebranch trees, his eyes tight shut.

Oliver was just about to perform his most daring stunt yet – a full-circle spin, while juggling six spell books – when he felt hot breath on his face.

"Ollie! No sleep!"

Oliver groaned and stirred. Oh, no! He'd been enjoying himself so much. Was it really only a dream?

He opened one eye a crack. His sister, the Witch Baby, was in front of his spiderweb hammock, bouncing a silver plastic teapot off his head. "Ollie! AWAKE," she ordered bossily.

Oliver shut his eye quickly, hoping he could finish his brilliant dream.

The alarm on his toad clock had other ideas though. "Eight o'croak," it burped, flicking a cold, wet tongue out onto Oliver's cheek. "Eight o'CROAK!"

Oliver groaned. Eight o'clock already!
He pulled his bat-blanket over his head.
He'd just lie here for a few more minutes...
THUMP!

"Ouch!" yelped Oliver, sitting up once more. The *Cacklewick Chronicle*, the local newspaper, had just materialized on top of his head. The *Chronicle* was *meant* to magically appear on the Moon family's doormat every morning, but it had the annoying habit of turning up in strange places all over the house.

Oliver rubbed his head crossly. No chance of getting back to sleep now. How he hated mornings!

"Cup tea," the Witch Baby said. She sloshed green slime from her teapot into a pink cup, and shoved it into Oliver's face. The slime splattered right into his mouth. Ugh! It stank! And it tasted vile!

Oliver grumpily reached for his dressing gown. As he did so, he caught sight of the *Chronicle*'s headline:

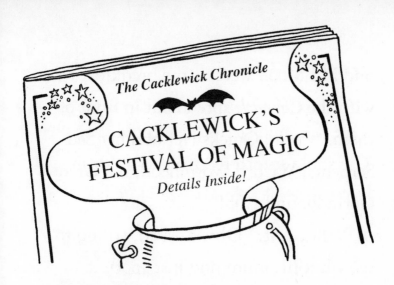

The Cacklewick Chronicle

CACKLEWICK'S FESTIVAL OF MAGIC

Details Inside!

"Cool!" Oliver breathed, forgetting his bad mood in an instant. The annual Festival of Magic was one of the most fantastic days of the whole year. He pulled on his dressing gown and rushed downstairs. "Mum, Dad!" he cried. "Come and look at this!"

"Ooh, have you *seen* who they've got lined up for the magical performances?" Mrs. Moon clucked, minutes later. She, Oliver and Mr. Moon were at the breakfast table with the *Chronicle* spread out in front of them. "Cecily Quicksilver and her Sea Serpents, Wizard Wormhead, the Great Gorindo, and…oh!"

"What is it?" Oliver asked, trying to see what his mum had just spotted.

His mum jabbed a finger at the newspaper, which promptly began to speak. "Rumour has it, there will be a special-guest appearance by the one and only Eliot Enchantrum!" the newspaper announced in a prim voice.

"Wow," Oliver breathed. Eliot Enchantrum was his hero – and the best wizard in the whole country!

"Eliot Smellipot," the Witch Baby commented loudly.

"A broomstick display by the Black Arrows, too," Mr. Moon read aloud. "Wonderful!"

"Firefly fireworks after dark, and live music from the Ravin' Ravens," Oliver added, feeling his skin prickle with excitement. The Ravin' Ravens were only his favourite band in the whole world!

"Nearly half past eight," the bearded grandfather clock suddenly warned, and Oliver jumped. He was still in his pyjamas!

16

Oliver ran upstairs and pulled on his school uniform and cloak. Then he grabbed his favourite wand and pointy hat and ran back down for breakfast.

Today might not have started off well – but with the magic festival just around the corner, things were definitely looking up!

Chapter Two

At Magic School that morning, Mrs. MacLizard, the head teacher, gathered all of the junior wizards and witches in the hall for assembly. "I'm sure you've all heard about this year's Festival of Magic," she said, beaming. "Well, it's my great pleasure to announce that this year, our school will be taking part in the grand parade."

There was a rustle of cloaks as everyone began whispering to one another. Oliver turned to his best friend, Jake Frogfreckle, his eyes bright. "Brilliant!" he hissed. "I—"

"CARK!" Mrs. MacLizard's raven screeched disapprovingly. It flew down from its roost on the curtain rail and swooped low over the heads of the students, knocking several pointy hats askew along the way.

The room fell silent at once. "Thank you, my little feather-flap," Mrs. MacLizard said, as the raven landed on her shoulder. It pecked at a beetle that was crawling through her hair and gulped it down. "Where was I? Oh, yes, the parade. You will all be split into groups," she went on. "And every group will have a team captain, who will choose a theme. You can have music,

costumes, and of
course, magic."
She smiled so
widely, Oliver
could see all
seven of her
stumpy
black teeth
on display.
"Let's make
the whole of
Cacklewick
proud of our
school!" she cried.

"Hooray!" the students all cheered,
Oliver included. He was gripping his
wand so tightly with excitement, that
it crackled a strange electric blue,

and sparks flew out of it like a firework. "This is going to be *fun*," Oliver laughed to Jake.

Mrs. MacLizard started dividing the school into teams. Merlin Spoonbender, the head wizard, was one of the captains, of course, as was Mabel Maldeval, the head witch. Oliver hoped he'd get put into either of their teams. They were both so awesome!

"Pippi Prowlcat, you're with Mabel,"
Mrs. MacLizard read from her list. "Jake
Frogfreckle, you're in Merlin's team…"

"YES!" cheered Jake, with an excited
smile. He got up and went over to Merlin's
team at once.

"Oliver Moon, you're in Snivel's team,"
Mrs. MacLizard said. "Boris Batbottom…"

Snivel's team? Oh. Oliver wasn't very
pleased about that. Snivel Mantis was
one of the prefects and kind of dull. Kind
of geeky, too. And very, very swotty.
Oliver sighed and got to his feet, just as
Bully Bogeywort, his worst enemy, barged
past him. "Looks like we're going to be
teammates," Bully sneered, his yellow
eyes smirking at Oliver. "Aren't you the
lucky one?"

Oliver's heart sank a little lower. In Snivel's team – with Bully Bogeywort? The parade had just become a lot less fun than it had sounded five minutes ago.

On the other side of the hall, Merlin's team were gathering. Already, Merlin was whirling his wand through the air and conjuring up a hovering picture of a fire-breathing red dragon. "This is what we're all going to build together, for the parade," Oliver heard him telling his team. They, of course, all looked wildly excited at the idea.

It's not fair, Oliver thought as he joined Snivel's group. Why had Jake been put in Merlin's team, and not him?

"Right, gang," Snivel said, twiddling his one and only beard bristle, "my idea for a theme is...potion-brewing."

"Du-ull," moaned Bully Bogeywort. For once, Oliver agreed.

Snivel ignored the interruption. "I will be dressed as a grandmaster wizard," he went on, his ears turning red at their tips, "and I will lead along a huge cauldron on wheels. You lot," he said, indicating the rest of the team, "are going to be my ingredients."

Oliver's shoulders slumped. Great. Knowing his luck, he'd end up as a dead bat. Whoopee-doo!

"Here's the really fun bit," Snivel said, his eyes gleaming. "Fun – *and* educational! As we're walking along, every time I wave my wand, one more ingredient jumps into the cauldron. So by the end of the parade, you'll all be in the cauldron together. Won't that be super?"

"What, so we won't get to see the rest of the parade once we're in the cauldron?" Hattie Toadtrumper asked, looking dismayed.

"That's right," Snivel said. "Affirmative. Er…yes." He beamed. "It'll be quite something, I think. Quite something indeed."

"Quite something *boring*, you mean,"
Bully Bogeywort muttered under
his breath.

Hattie rolled her eyes
at Oliver. Like they all
wanted to be stuck
in a dark cauldron
for the parade!
No way!

Snivel hadn't
finished. "Now,
as the wizard,
obviously I will be
the most important
person," he said, puffing out his skinny
chest. "And I thought it would look really
exciting if, every time I waved my wand,
red and purple smoke streamed out of it –

which then turned to red and purple paper stars." He paused as if he was expecting a round of applause at this suggestion. None came. "And then, what I was thinking, was that…"

Oliver found himself drifting off. It was bad enough being told that he was going to have to dress up as a boring ingredient for the parade. It was even worse having to listen to Snivel waffling on about *his* far more interesting part!

"…I think Oliver should do it," he heard Bully Bogeywort say suddenly. Oliver snapped out of his thoughts to see the rest of the team looking at him.

"Um…" Oliver mumbled, not wanting to admit he hadn't been listening.

"As it's such an important job, you

want somebody mature and sensible,"
Bully Bogeywort went on. "Like Oliver."

Snivel's beam was positively radiant.
"Oh, would you do that, Oliver? Would
you really?" he asked hopefully.

Oliver hesitated. What were they
talking about? He had
absolutely no idea. "Um…
okay," he agreed, crossing
his fingers. Surely
this important
job he was
agreeing to
couldn't be any
worse than being
a potion
ingredient,
could it?

"Smashing," Snivel said, clapping Oliver on the back. "We'll supply you with bin bags, of course. After all, litter collecting is *very* important."

Oliver's mouth dropped open in horror at Snivel's words. Litter collecting? Had he really just agreed to be a litter collector?

One look at Bully Bogeywort's smirk
told him the awful truth. Yes. There
would be no dressing up for him. No
jumping into a huge cauldron with all
the others. Instead, Oliver Moon would
be at the back of his team's procession,
picking up red and purple stars and
putting them in bin bags. Talk about
a rubbish job!

Chapter
Three

Oliver's mum and dad tried to cheer him
up at teatime that evening. "At least you
won't be stuck in a smelly old cauldron
for the whole parade," his mum said
encouragingly, ladling out a plateful of
toenail casserole.

"No, I'll just be carting smelly old bin
bags around instead," Oliver growled. He

stabbed his fork through a green potato and munched it crossly. "It's not fair. I wanted to be in Merlin's dragon team."

Oliver's dad passed him the pot of eyeballs. "Well, we're still proud of you, Oliver," he said. "I bet you'll be the finest litter collector in Cacklewick!"

Oliver pulled a face. Yeah, right. Like that was something to be proud of!

The next morning, Oliver was woken by a scorched smell. *Dad's burned the porridge again,* he thought sleepily, turning over in his hammock. But then his feet felt hot. Ouch! Really, really hot!

Oliver sat up and gulped in alarm. His hammock was on fire! "Help!" he yelped, leaping out of it, as the flames licked towards his toes. "FIRE!"

"Dragon," the Witch Baby said happily, pointing a podgy finger at a small green dragon with black smoke coming out of its nostrils.

The dragon burped, and breathed a huge jet of flames all over Oliver's pillow.

"Hey!" Oliver shouted, fumbling for his wand. "Bedroom rain... Put out flames!" he chanted, waving his wand over his hammock.

In an instant, rain began pouring from his bedroom ceiling. Oliver's hammock sizzled blackly where it had been burned. Oliver stood there, dripping wet, staring at the green dragon, which was now sheltering under one of its scaly wings.

The Witch Baby shrieked with excitement and danced about in the rain. "Garden," she said gleefully, patting the dragon. "Garden!"

"Spell – reverse! Before this gets worse!" Oliver said quickly, waving his wand. The rain stopped abruptly. "*Garden?*" he echoed, frowning at his sister. "What do you mean, garden?" He stared at the dragon. "Did you find the dragon in our garden?"

The Witch Baby's face split into a huge smile and she nodded. "MY dragon," she announced proudly. "Mine!"

"Cool!" Oliver said, as the dragon waddled out of his bedroom. "I've always wanted a family pet." A smile spread over his face. "Brilliant!"

But Oliver's excitement about the dragon didn't last long. "That dragon is *awful*!" he grumbled to Jake on the way to school that morning. "We were trying to teach it how to stoke up the cauldron for breakfast, but it managed to burn Dad's broomstick *and* Mum's dressing gown – and that was after setting fire to my bed!"

Jake chuckled. "Are your mum and dad going to let you keep it?"

Oliver shrugged. "Who knows? It's been banished to the garden for now. Dad's hoping it'll fly back to its own home. When I left, though, it was sulking in the nettles, trying to set fire to Mum's poison ivy plants." He shook his head at the thought. "I couldn't wait to get out of that madhouse and come to school."

"I couldn't wait either," Jake said. He bounced his skull football as they walked. "I am *so* looking forward to our next parade-team meeting. I spent all evening yesterday working on a design for our dragon's tail – that's the bit that Merlin's asked me to make," he added in a proud voice. "I thought I could build it out of…"

But Oliver had stopped listening. "That's it!" he declared, laughing out loud suddenly. "That's it!"

"That's what?" Jake echoed, looking puzzled.

Oliver grabbed Jake's skull football and bounced it off his own head. His pointy hat toppled off onto the pavement but he didn't even notice. "Jake, you've just given me the most excellent idea," he grinned. "Maybe litter collecting *will* be fun after all!"

Chapter
Four

Jake stared blankly at his friend. "How?" he asked doubtfully.

"I'll use the dragon!" Oliver exclaimed. "Instead of *me* picking up all the litter, the dragon can get rid of it by breathing fire on it! How cool will that be?"

"Red-hot!" Jake laughed. "You'll probably get your photo in the *Cacklewick*

Chronicle and everything. But…your dragon does sound a bit…wild. Do you think you'll be able to train it in time for the parade?"

Oliver hesitated. Ahh. Training the dragon. Somehow or other, he'd managed to forget that small point. He twirled his wand thoughtfully. "Well…" he began. He'd never had to train a dragon before. But surely it couldn't be that hard?

Bully Bogeywort came up just then, with a mean grin on his face. "Here you go," he said, emptying out his pockets in front of Oliver and Jake. A half-chewed frog bar fell out, and a mould-apple core. Some green snotty tissues fluttered down and a horrible lump of cloak fluff. "Now you can practise your litter collecting."

Then he guffawed so loudly, yellow spit flew out of his mouth like slimy rain.

Oliver wiped the spit out of his eyes, then folded his arms. "Actually, it won't be *me* picking up the litter in the parade after all," he couldn't resist saying rather boastfully. "My pet dragon will be getting rid of it for me."

Bully Bogeywort looked scornful. "You don't even have a pet dragon," he sneered.

"That's what *you* think," Oliver said, stepping over Bully's pile of litter. He turned and looked down pointedly at the messy pavement. "So you'd better pick up that lot yourself, hadn't you?"

After school that day, Jake came home with Oliver to give the dragon its first obedience lesson.

"Hopefully Mum and Dad have been able to teach it a few things already," Oliver said as they walked up the front path. "You wait, Jake. I'll have it trained in no time."

The house smelled very smoky, Oliver

thought, as they went through the front door, and there were several smouldering patches in the hall carpet, and smudgy soot marks on the ceiling. So the dragon had clearly been in the house recently – but where was it now?

"Dottie? She's in the garden," Oliver's mum told them, when they walked into the kitchen.

She was trying to mend the hole in her dressing gown with wool-worms, which kept wriggling out of her needle.

"Dottie?" Oliver echoed.

"That's what we've called her," his mum replied. "I was trying to teach her to roast some cockroaches for tea, but she set fire to the curtains by mistake." She glanced out of the window. "She's also burned the hall carpet, the living room carpet and your dad's new cloak, so I thought she'd be better off outside."

Oliver and Jake went into the garden. Dottie was up in the tanglebranch tree. She was wearing one of the Witch Baby's knitted bonnets on her head, and setting fire to some leaves with a moody expression on her face.

Under the tree, the Witch Baby had set up a tea party with some of her monster dolls. "Play," she was ordering the dragon, waving a teacup at her.

Dottie yawned and lost her balance, falling out of the tree and setting fire to the Witch Baby's picnic blanket as she did so.

Oliver quickly waved his wand to put out the flames, and took a deep breath. He had to go for it. He kneeled down in front of the dragon and looked into her glowing red eyes. "Hello, Dottie," he said, feeling a bit of an idiot. "I'm Oliver, okay? Your master. And I'm going to teach you a thing or two."

The dragon yawned again and a jet of flames roared out from between her sharp teeth. Oliver jumped back, his eyes smarting from the smoke.

"Good, that's it," he said encouragingly. "That's just what you have to do on the parade…when I tell you to. Not at any other time, though. So when I say, *Blast!*, I want you to breathe fire. Okay?"

Dottie scratched her side with sharp claws.

Oliver took that as a yes. He waved his wand to magic up some paper stars – "Twinkle papyro!" – and put them in a heap in front of the dragon. "There, look. Stars. See them?" he asked, prodding at them with his wand. "Are you ready? *Blast!*"

Dottie went on scratching, without even a glance at the stars.

"Er…Dottie?" Oliver said politely.

"Can you stop doing that for a second?
I'm trying to teach you something."

Dottie suddenly sneezed all over the
paper stars, coating them with thick
green droplets.

"Right," Oliver said. "Good try. And
again? *Blast!*"

Dottie began
picking at her
front claws,
cleaning
them with
her long
red tongue.

Oliver tried not to feel too downcast.
Dottie had been setting fire to things all
day by the sound of it, and the one time,
the *one time,* that somebody had actually
wanted her to breathe fire, she was more
interested in scratching and claw-
cleaning. Typical!

He looked over at Jake for
encouragement, but his friend was
looking doubtful. "You know, Ol – it was
a great idea to use a dragon in the

parade," Jake said slowly, "but…maybe not *this* dragon."

Oliver sighed. "Do you think I should forget the whole thing?" he asked.

Jake nodded. "Sorry, mate," he said, "but…"

Before Jake could finish his sentence, a messenger sprite suddenly materialized in the garden, in a thick cloud of stinky purple smoke. The sprite coughed and fanned away the smoke with a piece of parchment before announcing, "Message for Olivia Moo!"

"Moon," Oliver corrected him. "Oliver Moon."

The sprite frowned at the parchment before him. "Beg pardon," he said. "Magic writing is a mess sometimes. Message from Snivel Mantis: Heard about your...*dungeon* idea?"

"Dragon idea," Oliver said. How had Snivel found out about it? he wondered. Then he groaned, as he realized what had happened. Bully Bogeywort must have gone straight to Snivel to tell him – hoping to get Oliver in trouble, no doubt!

"Ahh yes. Heard about your *dragon* idea... Marvellous," the sprite went on. "Everyone will love it!"

His message delivered, the sprite promptly vanished leaving a curling wisp

of purple smoke that the Witch Baby
caught in her teacup and tried to drink.

Oliver and Jake exchanged worried
looks. "No going back now," Oliver said.
"If Snivel knows about my plan, he'll
have asked Mrs. MacLizard — and it
won't be long before *everyone* knows.
I can't say I've changed my
mind now." He sighed
as Dottie began
eating one of
the Witch
Baby's
monster
dolls. "That
dragon has
got to be
trained."

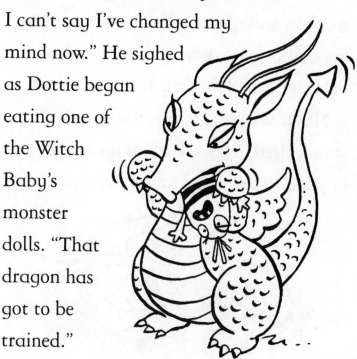

"Yes," Jake agreed, wincing at the Witch Baby's deafening squeal of rage. "But...how?"

Oliver turned and started back towards the house. "I don't know," he admitted. "Maybe..."

Oliver stopped as he heard a sudden rustling noise, and looked around hopefully. Was that the sound of flames licking through his paper stars?

No. It was not. It was the sound of a small, tired dragon curling up on a bed of paper stars...and falling asleep.

On Tuesday, Dottie *ate* the paper stars.

On Wednesday, Dottie hid in the paper stars.

On Thursday, Dottie did something yucky on the paper stars, and Oliver's mum made Oliver clean it up.

But on Friday, there was a breakthrough. Oliver magicked yet

another set of paper stars, and this time
the little dragon did actually set fire to
them. Unfortunately, the Witch Baby was
hiding in them at the time. "Naughty
Dottie!" she scolded as Oliver quickly cast
a rain spell over her. "Yucky Dottie!"

Oliver had quite gone off the dragon. The Witch Baby wasn't keen on her either. And his parents were all for finding her a new home. "I wish she'd just disappear back to wherever it was she came from," Mr. Moon said gloomily, eyeing the scorch marks on his favourite pointy hat.

But Oliver couldn't let Dottie go so easily. Because by now, everyone at Magic School had heard that she was going to be at the parade with Oliver. And everybody – even Mrs. MacLizard – had said how much they were looking forward to seeing her. He just had to go through with it!

*

The day of the parade dawned bright and sunny. As Oliver and Dottie set off after Wizard Snivel and his colossal cauldron, Oliver's tummy churned as if he'd eaten two hundred tentacles. *Please let Dottie behave!* he prayed.

The parade wove around the town centre and out into Cacklewick Park, through crowds of cheering witches and wizards. Merlin's team were up ahead with their realistic-looking red dragon – which was roaring so fiercely that Dottie was actually quite scared of it. Mabel's team were all dressed up as trolls, and singing a funny troll song together. There were white witches, shape-shifters and magic monsters. There was even a friendly giant stomping along, taking great care not to crush any of the festival-goers.

Whoosh! Snivel magicked the first stream of red and purple stars. They floated down through the air, sparkling in the sunshine.

"Blast!" Oliver told Dottie, as the stars rained down. *"Blast!"*

Dottie ignored the stars completely and trotted along, her nose in the air.

"Look, you stupid dragon, I said...
Oh, never mind." Sighing crossly, Oliver
snatched his pointy hat off his head and
stuffed a handful of stars into it. Why, oh
why, had he ever thought this would be a
good idea?

"Blast!" he ordered, pointing at another
pile of stars. Dottie singed Hattie
Toadtrumper's dung-beetle costume instead.

"Hey!" she squeaked from behind her mask. "Cut that out!"

"Sorry," Oliver sighed, stuffing more stars into his hat. He was starting to wish he'd brought along some bin bags after all. Dottie still hadn't burned a single star.

After a while, the parade made its way past the main Festival stage. All sorts of important-looking wizards and witches were preparing for their acts, testing their microphones were working, and warming up their wands.

Oliver felt quite star-struck as he spotted Cecily Quicksilver, one of the celebrity witches, setting up her basket of sea serpents at one side of the stage.

Wow! He was so close to her! Wait till he told his mum and dad!

Dottie seemed interested in Cecily Quicksilver, too. With a cheeky look

back at Oliver, she suddenly broke away
from the parade and flew up to the stage.

"Come back!" Oliver ordered, watching
her go in horror.

But it was too late. With a whoosh of
flames, the dragon had burned a hole in
Cecily's basket – and seconds later, the
sea serpents were escaping everywhere!

Chapter Six

Oliver could hardly bear to watch as the purple serpents swarmed quickly across the stage. "My babies! They're getting away!" Cecily Quicksilver screeched, her pointy hat falling off her head as she jigged up and down. "Whose is this dragon? Who is to blame for this?"

Her eyes fell upon Oliver, who was

trying to drag Dottie away from the stage. "She's mine," he confessed. "Sorry, she's—"

"You silly little wizard!" she spat at him. "My serpents are going everywhere!"

It was true. One serpent had slithered its way to the top of the stage curtains, where it dangled, like a long purple rope.

One serpent was sliding excitedly into

the crowd. People were backing away and screaming as it flicked its little black tongue out at them.

One serpent was even – oh, no! One serpent was wrapping itself around Mabel Maldeval's shoulders as she tried to lead her team through the parade. "Get off me, you overgrown worm!" she shouted, peeling it off herself and flicking it down to the ground.

"Ouch! It bit me!" came a voice from Wizard Snivel's cauldron, and a costumed cockroach came clambering out. A fourth sea serpent was firmly attached to the cockroach's bottom, clinging on by its fangs. Bully Bogeywort's yellow eyes looked frightened through his mask, as he wrestled the serpent off himself.

"Fancy being scared of a little snake," Hattie Toadtrumper said loudly, popping her head out of the cauldron and winking at Oliver.

Oliver nearly smiled back, but didn't dare with Cecily Quicksilver still glaring at him. "My focus…my creative energy…my preparation…shattered!" she wailed, waving her wand and chanting a beckoning spell to the serpents. "Now get that dragon away from me!" she bellowed.

Oliver picked up Dottie and tucked her under one arm. "Sorry," he mumbled to Cecily Quicksilver. Then he glared at Dottie. "Come on," he muttered through gritted teeth. "The parade is nearly over. Try to behave for the last bit – please!"

Oliver had never felt more relieved than when the parade was at an end. His pointy hat was absolutely stuffed with paper stars. His wand drooped wearily where it had put out so many of Dottie's fires with drenching spells. Dottie seemed tired, too. She didn't start a single fire as Oliver went to join his

family for the magical performances.
Hopefully she'd fall asleep, Oliver
thought to himself as she curled up on the
ground next to him. She couldn't cause
any trouble if she was asleep!

The show began and Oliver finally felt himself relax. Wizard Wormhead was wonderful. He turned himself into a rocket and flew up into space, then returned with a moon rock, two minutes later.

The Great Gorindo was…well, great. She turned her cat into a black dinosaur that took up the whole of the stage. Everybody gasped when the dinosaur picked up the Great Gorindo, and looked set to gobble her up.

But the witch calmly waved her wand.
With a flash of violet-coloured sparks,
the dinosaur turned back into a cat.

Cecily Quicksilver seemed a little flustered, unfortunately – and her sea serpents would not do a thing she commanded them to.

"That was your fault," Oliver hissed at Dottie, who blinked sleepily.

"And next," a voice boomed over the Tannoy, "flying in to make a special appearance at this year's Festival is the one and only…Eliot Enchantrum!"

The crowd cheered with excitement as, high up in the sky, a red dot became visible. Slowly the dot became larger and larger, and larger still, until the watching wizards and witches realized that Eliot Enchantrum was indeed flying in…on a huge red dragon!

The red dragon's wings beat powerfully through the air. There was Eliot Enchantrum on its back, waving at the crowd as his dragon swooped lower. And there was...

Oliver blinked and stared – then looked down at the space next to him where Dottie had been lying. Oh, no. There, in the sky, roaring with great excitement, was Dottie, flying towards the red dragon as fast as she could. So much for her falling asleep and staying out of trouble!

Oliver could hardly bear to watch. The dragons were sure to collide...and Eliot Enchantrum would fall off and injure himself...and there would be the most monumental fuss, and it would be *all his fault*!

His eyes closed, Oliver suddenly heard the crowd gasp – and then start clapping! He opened his eyes a crack to see Dottie flying gracefully behind the red dragon in a beautiful aerobatic display.

"Oooh," the crowd chorused as the dragons loop-the-looped six times in a row.

"Wow," they breathed, as the dragons flew smoothly backwards together.

"Hooray!" they cheered, as the dragons zigzagged through the clouds.

"Bravo!" they bellowed, clapping their hands and stamping their feet as both dragons landed on the main stage. Eliot Enchantrum leaped off the red dragon's back and went towards Dottie, who

gazed lovingly at him – then blew a
smoke ring…in the shape of a heart!

"Ahhh!" the audience sighed. Even
Oliver. He'd never seen Dottie look so
happy.

Eliot threw his arms around Dottie's
neck. "Doris! You're safe! We've been so

worried about you!" he cried happily.

Oliver's family stared at one another. *Doris?*

Eliot beamed at the audience. "Doris is the daughter of Daphne here," he said, patting the nose of the big red dragon. "And unfortunately for us, Doris wandered off and got lost when we were staying in Cacklewick the other week. We've been searching everywhere for her. I can't believe we've found her!"

Oliver's mouth hung open in surprise. To think that Dottie was really Eliot Enchantrum's dragon!

Dottie stayed onstage with the red dragon for the whole performance. She was as good as gold. She even helped with some of the spells.

"Why couldn't she be like that for us?" Mr. Moon complained in a whisper.

"Bless her," Mrs. Moon clucked, watching as Dottie trotted along the stage after the red dragon. "She was just missing her mummy."

At the end of Eliot's show, he hugged both the dragons. "I'd like to thank Cacklewick Council for asking me to the Festival of Magic this year," he said. A huge cheer went up. "And I'd also like to thank whoever was looking after Doris for me, while she was lost," he went on. "She's clearly been looked after very well."

"It was us!" Oliver shouted, waving a hand.

"Our pleasure!" Mrs. Moon said, beaming.

Mr. Moon stared at her as if she was mad. "Our *pleasure?*" he echoed in a disbelieving mutter. "That's not what I would call it."

"Thank you," Eliot called out to the Moons, and a handful of free tickets to Eliot Enchantrum's next show appeared in Oliver's hand amid a flurry of magical sparkles.

Then Eliot waved to the audience. "Goodbye, everyone! Enjoy the rest of the Festival!" And the dragons flew up into the sky again, with Eliot on the red dragon's back.

"Bye-bye," the Witch Baby said, waving a fat hand at the sky.

Oliver smiled in delight as he tucked the tickets into his cloak. What a result!

The rest of the Festival was fantastic. The
Ravin' Ravens were awesome, as was the
Black Arrows' display. Everyone had a
wonderful time.

"It's time to go home now," Mrs. Moon

said, as the last act finished.

Oliver and his family drifted through the Festival grounds, past the stalls and sideshows which were all closing up.

The Witch Baby suddenly broke free from Mrs. Moon's hand and toddled to one of the stalls. "Want that!" she shrieked urgently. "Want THAT!"

Oliver looked to see what his sister had spotted — and groaned. She was standing in front of a magical pets stall, pointing excitedly at a very grumpy-looking griffin.

"Want that!" the Witch Baby repeated. "Want it!"

Mr. Moon shuddered. "No chance," he said firmly. "One pet disaster is enough for this family, thank you very much!"

BEASTLY BUSINESS

Oliver put an arm around his sister. "Come on," he said. "If you're really good, I'll get you one of those hairy spiders for Christmas instead."

The Witch Baby gave Oliver a slobbery kiss on the cheek. "Nice Ollie," she said. "Ta."

"You're welcome," Oliver said, steering her well away from the griffin. "Let's go home now."

And they did.

The End

Oliver Moon
Junior Wizard

Collect all of Oliver Moon's magical adventures!